THE TREASURE TROOP

Summer Island

by Dori Hillestad Butler
illustrated by Tim Budgen

Penguin Workshop

For Michele, my colleague, friend, and writing partner, who loves games, puzzles, and the Pacific Northwest as much as I do–DHB

To friendship, teamwork, and adventure–TB

PENGUIN WORKSHOP
An Imprint of Penguin Random House LLC, New York

Text copyright © 2021 by Dori Hillestad Butler. Illustrations copyright © 2021 by Penguin Random House LLC. All rights reserved. Published by Penguin Workshop, an imprint of Penguin Random House LLC, New York. PENGUIN and PENGUIN WORKSHOP are trademarks of Penguin Books Ltd, and the W colophon is a registered trademark of Penguin Random House LLC. Printed in Canada.

Visit us online at www.penguinrandomhouse.com.

Library of Congress Cataloging-in-Publication Data
is available upon request.

ISBN 9780593094884 (pbk)   10 9 8 7 6 5 4 3 2 1
ISBN 9780593094891 (hc)   10 9 8 7 6 5 4 3 2 1

Chapter 1

STRANGE OBJECT

"Keep a lookout for whales," Captain Joe called from the boat's wheelhouse. "You might spot one right in here."

"Really?" Marly Deaver squealed. She and her friends, Isla Thomson and Sai Gupta, rushed to the railing. All around them, evergreen-covered islands rose from the water like giant tortoises. Wind whipped through their hair.

Marly squinted, but as usual everything looked blurry. She had one pretty good eye,

1

but she wore a patch over it to try to train her bad eye to work better. It was so frustrating to not be able to see as well as everyone else.

"See any whales?" Marly asked Isla and Sai.

"Not yet." Sai curled his fingers like they were binoculars and peered through them.

Isla grabbed her cat ear headband before it blew off her head. "Me neither."

"The captain says to look for a fin or a spray of water or even something that looks like a giant rock floating on the surface," Ms. Lovelace said, joining them on deck.

Marly slid her patch onto the rim of her glasses and scanned the water. She wanted so badly to see a whale.

Ms. Lovelace touched Marly's shoulder. "I promised your mom I wouldn't let you take that patch off," she said.

Marly sighed. "I know," she grumbled, sliding the patch back into place. She'd promised her mom the same thing.

This trip was Marly's first time away from home without her family. Isla and Sai's, too. It was weird to think about how they had hardly known each other at the beginning of the summer, and now they were the best of friends.

It was all thanks to Marly's next-door neighbor, Mr. Summerling. Isla and Sai had both known him, too. Unfortunately, he had passed away at the beginning of the summer.

"I wonder if Mr. Summerling ever saw a whale," Isla said.

"Probably," Sai said.

"He probably saw lots of things we've never seen," Marly said. Mr. Summerling used to travel all over searching for buried treasure. In fact, that was how he'd died. Marly gulped as she realized that what happened to Mr. Summerling had probably happened somewhere around *here*.

He'd been exploring some Pacific Northwest islands when a storm came up.

The coast guard found his boat drifting upside down, but Mr. Summerling himself was nowhere to be found. The coast guard said he probably drowned.

Marly shaded her eye and gazed up at the sky. She was relieved there were no storm clouds today.

Marly, Isla, and Sai had found out about Mr. Summerling's death a few weeks ago when Ms. Lovelace called them to her office to read his will. Ms. Lovelace was Mr. Summerling's attorney. In his will, Mr. Summerling had left a treasure hunt for his eight-year-old friends. They ran all over town solving puzzles until they finally found the treasure, which turned out to be a tree house in the woods behind his and Marly's houses.

Then, just last week, they'd uncovered a secret message hidden beneath a floorboard in the tree house. That message was the beginning of a second treasure hunt, which led them through hidden doors and secret passageways inside Mr. Summerling's house, finally ending with an invitation to a place called Summer Island.

Marly still couldn't believe their parents had let them come. Summer Island was two thousand miles from home. But Ms. Lovelace had been very persuasive, and she'd promised to look after the kids as though they were her own.

Marly felt both excited and nervous about this trip. Mostly excited. There was obviously going to be one more treasure hunt, and Marly couldn't wait to see the first clue.

"That's Summer Island straight ahead." Captain Joe pointed. He wore a white hat and had a toothpick sticking out of the side of his mouth.

The kids moved to the front of the boat. Funny, when Marly first heard about this place, she'd pictured an island with flat sandy beaches, palm trees, and lots of sun. But like most of the other islands they'd passed, the shore ahead looked rocky rather than sandy. The island was blanketed in tall evergreens rather than palm trees. And though the sun was out, there was enough of a chill in the air that everyone was wearing jackets.

"How big is that island, anyway?" Marly turned toward Captain Joe. The railing vibrated beneath her hands.

Captain Joe cupped a hand to his ear. It was hard to hear over the sound of the boat. So Marly repeated her question. Louder this time.

"'Bout eight square miles," Captain Joe said.

"What does that mean?" Sai shouted. "Could you walk around the whole island?"

Captain Joe shrugged. "You could. But it would take a while." He moved the toothpick to the other side of his mouth. "Better to bike around it."

"We don't have bikes," Isla said. They'd

each brought a suitcase and Marly had her
metal detector. But they didn't have anything
else. Ms. Lovelace had told them they'd be
staying in a large cabin and everything they
needed, including food, would be there.

"How many people live on this island?" Ms. Lovelace asked.

"None," Captain Joe said as he slowed the boat.

"None?" Marly, Isla, and Sai said at the same time.

"I'm sure there are people who have cabins and spend time there during the summer," Ms. Lovelace said.

"Not anymore," Captain Joe said. "Far as I know, Harry Summerling is the only one who has a place here now."

"You mean we're going to be the only people on the whole island?" Marly asked. She wasn't sure how she felt about that.

But Sai seemed excited. "Cool!" he said, rubbing his hands together. Isla bit her lip and fiddled with her bee sting allergy bracelet. Ms. Lovelace's expression gave nothing away.

"Did you know Mr. Summerling?" Isla asked Captain Joe.

"Of course," he replied. "Harry and I go way back. I'm the one who first showed him these islands." He slowed the boat even more and steered toward a large dock. There was a tiny bump as the boat came to rest along a line of old tires that were fastened to the side of the dock.

"Here we are!" Captain Joe left the motor running while he tied the boat to a metal cleat. Everyone else gathered up their things.

Captain Joe set out a small stool, and one by one, Sai, Marly, Isla, and Ms. Lovelace climbed up onto the dock.

"I hope you all enjoy your time here as much as Harry did," Captain Joe said, tipping his hat.

"I'm sure we will," Ms. Lovelace replied. "Now, where's the cabin?" She turned toward shore and shaded her eyes. "I thought it would be right at the end of the dock." There were no buildings in sight. Only trees.

9

Captain Joe gestured toward a narrow dirt path that led uphill into the trees. "Just follow the path. You'll come to a driveway," he said.

"And you'll be back for us Monday morning?" Ms. Lovelace said.

Captain Joe nodded once. "Eight a.m. sharp."

Monday was four days from now.

"Let's go!" Sai grabbed his suitcase and charged toward shore.

Ms. Lovelace, Isla, and Marly followed at a slower pace, the dock swaying a little beneath them.

"Wait! I almost forgot," Captain Joe called. Marly hung back while he ducked inside the wheelhouse and returned with a strange stick. It was about three feet long, maybe an inch thick, and it looked like someone had whittled it smooth. "You'll need this." He handed it to Marly.

"For what?" she asked, turning it all around.

Captain Joe didn't answer. He just smiled mysteriously as he untied the boat. Then he returned to the wheel and motored away.

Chapter 2

HARRY5

"What is that?" Isla walked back toward Marly.

"Some kind of stick," Marly said, still wondering about it herself.

"Yeah, but what's it for?" Isla asked.

Marly shrugged. "The captain didn't say. He just said we'd need it."

"Come on, girls!" Ms. Lovelace waved to them from shore. Sai was already halfway up the hill. The wheels on his suitcase kicked up clouds of dust behind him.

Marly tucked the stick into the front pocket of her suitcase, grabbed her metal detector, and clomped up the dock with Isla. Even when they set foot on land, Marly felt like she was still rocking on a boat.

She followed Isla and Ms. Lovelace up the steep dirt path, her chest heaving with the effort. Tall moss-covered trees towered over them, blocking out the sun.

"Uh . . . there's no house or cabin up here," Sai called down from the top of the hill.

"There must be," Ms. Lovelace called back. "Look around."

But when Ms. Lovelace, Isla, and Marly reached Sai, they discovered he was right. There was nothing up here but trees. And another dirt path. This one was wider than the one that led down to the dock. They could all stand side by side on it.

"Maybe *this* is the path we're supposed to follow," Marly said.

"Okay, but which way?" Isla asked.

Ms. Lovelace looked equally confused. "Let's try this way." She made a wide turn with her suitcase toward the right. "If we don't come to the cabin, we'll turn around and go the other way."

They walked in silence, their suitcases bumping behind them. Birds chirped, and the group heard water lapping at the shore, but they couldn't see it through the thick trees.

Marly switched her suitcase and metal detector between her hands. Man, she was tired. Not just tired of walking and carrying her stuff, but tired in general. It had been a long day. They'd had an early flight to Seattle. Then a long boat ride. Plus a two-hour time change. And now it was so dark beneath all these trees that it just made Marly feel even more tired.

"Okay," Ms. Lovelace said, after several minutes. "Let's try the other way."

The view was the same in this direction. Trees, trees, and more trees. The path got a little brighter as they passed the hill that led down to the boat dock. They kept going.

"Hey, there's a driveway," Sai said, hurrying ahead.

"Slow down," Ms. Lovelace called to him. But "slow down" was not in Sai's vocabulary. He didn't slow down until he reached the driveway. There he waited for everyone else to catch up.

"Do you see the cabin?" Isla asked.

"No." Sai peered through the gap in the trees. "But it's a *looong* driveway."

"Are you sure that's a driveway?" Marly asked, stopping beside Sai. If it was, no one had driven on it in a long time. Tall weeds sprouted up in the middle of it.

"Looks like a driveway to me," Ms. Lovelace said. "Come on." She tromped right through the weeds, and the kids followed close behind, winding through more forest until they finally came to an old rundown garage. There had clearly been a house beside the garage at one time, but all that was left of it now was part of a broken concrete foundation. They all stared at it in dismay.

"I hope this isn't where we were supposed to stay," Isla said.

"No," Ms. Lovelace said. "I've seen pictures of Harry's cabin. It's beautiful. It's nestled in the woods and it's got a nice big porch."

There was nothing like that anywhere around.

"We don't have a car, so it's got to be within walking distance of the dock," Ms. Lovelace went on. "I'll call Captain Joe back and get more specific directions." She reached into her purse and pulled out her phone.

Sai went over to the broken foundation, climbed up on it, and started walking along it like it was a balance beam.

"Careful, Sai," Isla warned him.

Marly wandered over to the garage. She tried the handle on a side door. She was surprised to find it unlocked!

"Oh no!" Ms. Lovelace stared at her phone. "I don't have any cell service."

Isla's eyes grew wide with worry. "What? We're alone on this island. We don't know where the cabin is. There's no transportation. And we can't even call anyone? What are we going to do?"

Marly pushed the door to the garage all the way open and poked her head inside. "Well, there's some kind of vehicle in here," she told the others.

Sai jumped down and hurried over. "It's like an army car," he said, crowding in next to Marly. The vehicle was completely open on the sides and the top.

Marly flipped a switch beside the door and a dim bulb on the ceiling came on as they all stepped inside the garage. It was full of cobwebs and rusty old tools.

"It's an ATV," Ms. Lovelace said, checking it out.

"Maybe it's for us!" Sai exclaimed.

Isla brushed a cobweb from her shoulder. "We can't drive," she said.

"Ms. Lovelace can," Sai said.

"I don't know." Ms. Lovelace scratched her head. "We can't just take a vehicle we found in some abandoned garage."

"Why not? It's probably Mr. Summerling's," Sai said. "Captain Joe said no one else has a place on this island." He leaned into the vehicle through the open passenger-side window.

Marly walked around behind it. "It *is* Mr. Summerling's," she said. "The license plate says 'HARRY5.'"

Isla twirled her hair around her finger. "We still don't know where the cabin is," she pointed out. "So where would we drive to?"

"Captain Joe told us to follow the path," Marly said. "Maybe we're supposed to follow it in this." She patted the side of the vehicle.

Ms. Lovelace tried the driver's door. It opened! "We need a key if we're going to go anywhere," she said. "I've got one for the cabin, but not for this."

Sai climbed into the front passenger seat. "There's a glove box." He opened it and pulled out a map, an extremely long, narrow strip of paper . . . and a key. "Aha!" he cried, raising the key in his fist.

"What's all that other stuff?" Marly asked.

"Hang on," Sai said, stuffing everything but the key back inside the glove box. "Let's see if this thing starts before we look at anything else." He leaned over and handed the key to Ms. Lovelace.

She went to open the big garage door, then got into the driver's seat. She tried to

wiggle the key into the ignition, then gave up.
"Unfortunately, this isn't the right key," she
said, holding it up. "It doesn't fit the ignition."

Chapter 3

LOST

"Then why was it in the glove box?" Marly asked.

"Good question," Sai said. He got out of the ATV and slammed the door.

"What else was in the glove box?" Isla asked.

Sai reached back in through the window and opened it. "A map," he said, pulling it out. "And this weird strip of paper." He raised it high above his head. It hung all the way to the ground.

Isla took the map and Marly picked up the

bottom end of the strange strip of paper. She stretched it out between her and Sai. "What *is* this?" she asked. It was only as wide as her finger, but it was really long. Longer than she was tall. One side was blank. The other side had a single line of capital letters running the entire length of it.

"Looks like a puzzle!" Sai said.

"It does," Marly agreed, though all their other puzzles had been written on *From the Desk of Harry P. Summerling* stationery. Still, what else could this be? She started reading letters from her end of the paper out loud. "'*B, T, R, Y*—'"

Isla interrupted her. "Hey, let's find the cabin before we start talking about puzzles, okay?" She opened the map.

"Maybe we have to solve this puzzle in order to find the cabin," Marly said.

"Wait a minute," Ms. Lovelace said, opening her purse again. "It's a long shot, but I wonder if the key that I thought was for the cabin is actually for the ATV." She took out a plain old ordinary key. It had a piece of tape on it that said Island Key.

Sai shrugged. "Let's see."

Ms. Lovelace got into the vehicle. She slipped the key into the ignition, and this time the vehicle roared to life. Marly, Isla, and

Sai cheered and backed away as Ms. Lovelace slowly drove out of the garage.

"Good thinking, Ms. Lovelace!" Sai exclaimed. Marly shoved the strip of paper into her jacket pocket and went to get her stuff.

Ms. Lovelace blushed. "You know what?" she said. "We're going to be spending a lot of time together over the next four days. Why don't you all call me Stella."

Stella left the ATV running while they piled their suitcases into the back. Marly laid her metal detector on top. Then they all climbed back in. Once everyone was buckled up, Stella drove slowly down the long tree-lined driveway.

She stopped when she reached the "road" where they'd been walking before. It was almost wide enough to be called a road. "Which way?" she asked. "Anyone want to guess?"

Isla peered at the map. "Believe it or not, this road is called Main Path. It goes around the whole island."

"That's creative," Marly said, leaning over so she could see the map, too.

"Hey, Mr. Summerling had a copy of this map hanging in his dining room," Marly said.

"Weird," Sai said.

Marly tried to remember if the two maps were exactly the same or whether the cabin

was marked on the map at Mr. Summerling's house. She couldn't recall.

"How about I pick a direction and see what we find?" Stella said. She turned left, which was away from the boat dock. "Can you all help me watch for side trails and driveways?"

"Sure!" Isla and Sai leaned their heads out their open windows.

But Marly's eyesight was so poor, she wasn't sure how much help she could be. "Maybe I should work on the puzzle," she said, pulling it out of her pocket.

Sai turned around from the front seat. "If you're going to work on the puzzle, I want to help," he said.

"Okay." Marly handed him one end of the paper and they stretched it out as best they could between the front seat and back seat.

"Careful you don't tear it." Isla's brow wrinkled.

They came to a fork in the road and Stella

stopped driving. A wooden sign pointed to another path that veered off to the side: Wooded Trail. "Isla, do you see Wooded Trail on that map?"

Sai let go of his end of the paper and peered out the window. "How is that trail any more wooded than the trail we're already on?" he asked.

Marly was wondering the same thing. This whole island seemed to be nothing but woods.

"No Wooded Trail," Isla said, raising her head. "There's a Lost Trail, a Raven Trail, and a Deer Lane."

"Deer Lane?" Marly said. "Do you think there are really deer on this island?"

"Could be," Stella said as she continued driving. "I think I remember Harry talking about deer."

All of a sudden, Isla cried, "Stop!"

"What?" Stella slammed on the brakes.

"Sorry. Not you, Stella," Isla said. "I meant

Marly. Stop twirling that paper."

Marly blinked in surprise. She hadn't realized she had been twirling it. But somehow, most of her finger was wrapped in the paper. She started to unwind it—

"No, don't unwind it. Not yet!" Isla put her hand over Marly's hand. "There's a word on your finger."

Marly frowned. "There is? Where?" But then she saw it. "'*L-O-S-T*,'" she read, touching each of the letters.

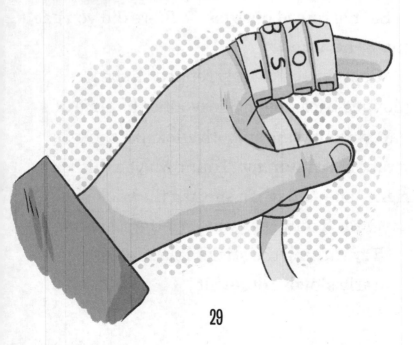

"Yeah, we're lost all right," Sai grumbled.

Isla grinned. "I think I know how to solve the puzzle," she said. "We need to wrap the paper around something. Something that's longer than your finger."

"Oh!" Marly said eagerly. "I know what we can wrap it around." She carefully removed the paper from her finger. Then she unfastened her seatbelt and climbed up onto her knees so she could reach her suitcase and get the stick that she'd tucked into the front pocket.

Sai narrowed his eyes. "Where did you get that?" he asked

"Captain Joe," Marly replied as she plopped back down. She wound the strip of paper around the smooth stick like she was wrapping a mummy. "Hmm. Maybe this *isn't* right," she said when she had the stick half covered. "I only see random letters. No words."

"Try turning the stick," Isla said.

Marly slowly rotated it.

"There!" Isla cried, her finger shooting out. "See? There's *LOST* again."

The lines of letters still weren't totally straight, but they were straight enough to spell words. "'LOST TRAIL TO,'" Marly read.

"Keep winding," Isla said, jiggling Marly's elbow.

Marly wound the rest of the paper as fast as she could. Once she finished, the full message appeared: LOST TRAIL TO BUNNY TRAIL.

Chapter 4

CABIN IN THE WOODS

"So, finding the cabin really is our first puzzle," Sai said, rubbing his hands together.

"And this strip of paper was our first clue," Marly said.

Isla pored over the map. "I see a Lost Trail," she said, tossing her hair over her shoulder. "But no Bunny Trail."

"Well, let's find Lost Trail," Stella said. "Then we'll worry about Bunny Trail. Buckle up, Marly."

Marly fastened her seatbelt, and Stella started driving again.

The girls checked the map. "Shouldn't be much farther," Isla said. "It'll be a right turn."

"Harry left a lot of instructions for this trip, but somehow he forgot to mention the ATV or how to find the cabin," Stella grumbled.

"When did he leave you instructions?" Sai asked.

"It was in a letter that I opened right after I gave you the envelope that started you on the treasure hunt inside Harry's home," Stella said. "Remember? I had several letters from Harry."

Marly remembered. They'd seen those extra envelopes both times they'd visited Stella's office.

"Harry left specific instructions for when each one was to be opened and by whom," Stella explained. "The one that was addressed to me told me what I was supposed to do when you found the tickets to Summer Island. And I had no doubt you'd find them quickly. So, as soon as you left, I closed up my office and started making arrangements for this trip. Harry's letter told me how to get in touch with Captain Joe, and the captain told me everything I needed to know about the cabin. Except, apparently, how to get there." She looked a little frustrated.

Isla leaned forward in her seat. "It's okay. We found the ATV. We'll find the cabin, too."

"I think Mr. Summerling liked to turn whatever he could into a puzzle," Marly said. "He knew we'd figure it out."

Soon they came to a wooden sign that read Lost Trail. Stella turned onto another dark and narrow path. It was barely wide enough for the ATV.

She stopped a few minutes later. "Another fork in the road," she announced. "But no sign saying what this trail is called."

"Then let's keep going," Isla said, her eyes focused on the map. "Maybe there will be a sign for Bunny Trail like the one we saw for Wooded Trail."

Stella kept driving. A little farther down the path, they did indeed come to another wooden sign.

"'Bunny Trail'!" Sai cried, reading the sign out loud.

Stella turned onto Bunny Trail and followed it around a bend where the path opened up into a wide clearing. And there, standing in the setting sun, was a beautiful log cabin with a wide front porch.

Stella stopped the ATV and leaned back against her seat. "Now, *that's* what I expected Harry's cabin to look like," she said.

Everyone got out of the vehicle and Marly, Isla, and Stella began to gather their things from the back. Sai raced straight up the steps to the cabin. He opened the screen door,

then let it fall shut again. "Door's locked," he said, running back to get his suitcase.

"Of course it is," Isla said with a sigh. "Do we have another key?"

"Well, there's the one Sai found in the glove compartment. I've got it right here." Stella patted her front pocket as they tromped up the stairs. Stella inserted that key into the lock and turned the handle. The door opened!

"Hooray!" the kids cheered.

"Wow, this is nice," Isla said as they stepped into the living room.

The walls were made of smooth, thick logs. Marly couldn't resist touching one. There was a large stone fireplace, a sofa, two chairs, and a cabinet with a TV in the main room. Beyond the fireplace was a small kitchen, a bedroom, and a bathroom.

"There should be two more bedrooms up there." Stella gestured toward an open loft above them.

"Do we get to sleep up there?" Sai asked.

"You do," Stella said.

"Yes!" Sai raised his fist in the air.

Marly set her metal detector by the door and the kids hauled their suitcases upstairs. There was a cozy sitting area at the top of the landing. It had a small couch, three bookshelves, and a railing where they could look down on the main floor of the cabin. Off to the left were two small bedrooms and a bathroom.

Marly and Isla claimed the bedroom with the twin beds, leaving Sai with the smaller bedroom.

Sai didn't bother to unpack. "I'm starving," he said from the railing. "Can we get dinner?"

"Absolutely," Stella replied. "Then I think we should all go to bed. We've had a long day. And I know you'll have some puzzles to solve in the morning."

"Can we get our next clue tonight?" Sai

asked as Marly and Isla joined him at the railing.

Stella looked confused. "Your next clue?"

"Don't you have our next clue?" Sai asked.

"Not that I'm aware of," Stella replied. "I didn't have the first clue, either, remember?"

Marly, Isla, and Sai exchanged looks. *If Stella doesn't have our next clue, where is it?*

Considering how tired she was, Marly had a hard time falling asleep that night. She wasn't sure if it was the strange bed, or maybe a bit of homesickness, or both.

She rolled over and squinted into the darkness. She didn't have to wear her patch at night, but it was too dark to see anything in here anyway.

"Psst," she hissed at Isla. "You awake?"

Isla didn't respond.

Marly lay back on her pillow and sighed. She wondered if Sai was awake.

She got out of bed and crept out into the sitting area. Stella had left a kitchen light on downstairs, but her bedroom door was closed. Judging from the loud snores coming from Sai's room, he was asleep, too.

It wasn't any fun being the only one awake. But since she was up, Marly wandered into the bathroom. She closed the door and turned on the light. After using the toilet, she washed her hands and started to dry them on a towel that hung on the rack, but it felt damp.

There have to be other towels in here somewhere. Marly opened the cabinet behind the door and found a whole pile of them, as well as some extra soaps, shampoos, and bubble bath. As she started to close the door, a paper stuck to the inside caught her eye. The top, bottom, and left side of the paper were cut straight, but the right side had been cut at weird angles.

There were no words on the paper. No *From the Desk of Harry P. Summerling* at the top, either. But the whole page was full of little groupings of dots.

Marly grinned. It had to be another puzzle. Too bad Isla and Sai were fast asleep.

Chapter 5

DOTS... DOTS... DOTS...

In the morning, Marly was eager to show Isla and Sai the paper she'd found during the night. But when she got up, they were already downstairs. She dressed quickly and hurried down to join them.

Stella was frying bacon and eggs at the stove. Isla was setting the table. And Sai was watching the toaster. But as soon as Marly entered the room, he looked up and waved a piece of paper at her. It had three straight edges and one jagged edge. And the writing

43

was all dots. "Look what I found!" he said.

"It's our next puzzle," Isla told Marly.

"Yeah, I found it, too," Marly said. "During the night. But I left it so you two could see where it was."

Isla blinked in surprise. "You made toast during the night?" she asked.

"What? No," Marly said, confused. "Why?"

"Because the clue was in the toaster," Sai said, as though it were obvious. "It looks like dominoes, don't you think?" He held the paper up so they could all see it.

"I think it looks like Legos," Isla said.

"Wait," Marly said. "I found that same clue in the bathroom. Not the toaster."

Marly ran back upstairs and opened the cabinet behind the bathroom door. The paper was still there! She carefully untaped it and brought it back downstairs.

"Looks like there are two clues," she said, bringing the paper to Sai. The papers

appeared identical at first glance, but the
pattern of dots was different.

"Oh! Maybe they fit together like a puzzle,"
Sai said. He tried to line up his paper with
Marly's, but the jagged edges didn't match up.

"It's the same kind of code on both papers,

though," Isla said, looking on.

"Breakfast time," Stella said. She set a bowl of eggs and a plate of bacon on the table. "Why don't you put those papers on the counter so you don't accidentally spill food on them."

"Aww," Sai groaned. But he did as Stella asked, and they all sat down at the table.

"Are you going to help us with the treasure hunt, Stella?" Isla asked as she passed the eggs to Marly.

"No." Stella shook her head. "Harry said I work too hard, so while you're off solving puzzles and searching for treasure, I'm supposed to 'relax.'" She made air quotes around the word.

"He gave us a treasure hunt and he gave you a vacation!" Sai said, reaching for a slice of toast.

"Except for taking care of us," Marly said.

"That shouldn't be too hard." Stella smiled.

"I think I'll have plenty of time to sit and read on that nice front porch."

"What happens if we don't find the treasure by Monday?" Isla asked, concerned.

"We go home without it," Stella said.

Marly, Isla, and Sai exchanged worried glances.

"Do you know what the treasure is this time?" Marly asked.

"I do not," Stella replied.

"Let's hurry up," Sai said, shoveling his breakfast in. "We need to get going on the puzzle."

"So, each 'letter' is a group of up to six dots," Isla said as she, Marly, and Sai sat in a line on the sofa and studied the papers.

Marly opened the notebook they'd been using to solve all the other puzzles and

flipped to a fresh page. But until they figured
out what to do with this puzzle, she didn't
have anything to write.

"What kind of puzzle is all dots?" Sai asked.

"Can you draw lines between the dots and
form letters?" Isla suggested.

Marly tried tracing a few different paths through the dots with the eraser end of her pencil. She found an *L* and a backward *C*, but nothing that formed actual words.

"Wait a minute," Marly said, sitting up a little straighter. "I did a report on Helen Keller last year. She was blind and deaf, and she read braille. I'm pretty sure that every letter in braille has up to six dots."

"Yeah, but don't you read braille with your fingers?" Isla asked. She ran a finger over one of their papers. "I can't feel these dots at all."

"Still could be braille," Marly said.

"Do either of you know braille?" Sai asked. "Because I sure don't."

"No," Marly said. Isla shook her head. "We could look it up, though." Marly turned all the way around on the sofa. "Hey, Stella?"

"Yes?" Stella looked over. She was cleaning up the kitchen.

"I know you didn't have cell phone service

when we first got to this island, but do you have it now?" Marly asked. "We need to get on the internet so we can look up the braille alphabet."

"Sorry," Stella said. "I checked last night. No cell service and no Wi-Fi. That means no internet."

The kids groaned.

"How are we going to solve this without the internet?" Sai slumped back against the sofa cushion.

"I knew Harry pretty well," Stella said. "I'd be surprised if you needed the internet to solve any of his puzzles. Whatever you need is probably right here in this cabin."

Chapter 6

PUTTING PIECES TOGETHER

Marly, Isla, and Sai scanned the bookshelves in the upstairs sitting area. They were on the lookout for something, anything, that could contain the braille alphabet.

"Hey, encyclopedias!" Marly exclaimed. "That's like the internet in book form."

Isla grabbed the *B* book and started flipping pages. "Here we go. 'Louis Braille.' And look!" She held the book so Marly and Sai could see it. There was a small chart of the braille alphabet at the bottom of the page.

Sai picked up one of their papers of dots and held it next to the chart. "It *is* braille!" he exclaimed. "See? The first letter is an *H*." He pointed back and forth between the first character on the paper and the *H* on the braille chart.

"It is?" Marly said, squinting at it.

"Can I have a pen or pencil?" Sai asked, holding out his hand.

Marly reached into her tote bag and pulled out both. Sai took the pencil, and he and Isla sat down on the floor with the two papers and the encyclopedia. Marly sat down beside them.

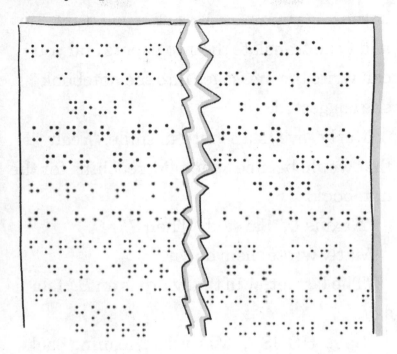

"Second letter is an *O*," Isla said. Sai put an *O* beneath the second set of dots.

Marly squinted again. It was hard for her to see those small dots. "This is going to take forever," she said as she rubbed her unpatched eye. They'd only done two letters. There were at least fifty to go on the first paper, and then there was a whole other paper to do.

Isla glanced at her curiously. "Are the dots bothering your eyes, Marly? If you want, Sai and I can translate the two papers and you can write the messages into the notebook," she suggested.

Marly gave Isla a grateful smile. "Yeah, that would be nice," she said, reaching for the notebook.

"Next is *U*," Sai said. "Then *S*."

Marly wrote them down.

"The last letter in that word is an *E*," Isla said.

"So . . . HOUSE," Marly said, leaning back against the small couch. "Keep going."

They did. And twenty minutes later they had all the words on the first paper decoded: HOUSE, YOUR STAY, BIKES, THEY ARE, WHILE YOU'RE, DOWN, BEACH DON'T, AND METAL, GET TO, YOURSELVES AT, and SUMMERLING.

Sai wrinkled his nose. "That doesn't make sense. Do we have to rearrange the words, too?"

"Let's do the other paper," Isla said. "Then we can figure out what comes next."

"Okay," Sai said.

He and Isla went back to work, comparing each new set of dots to the chart in the encyclopedia while Marly wrote their translations in the notebook.

When they finished with the second paper, they had: WELCOME TO, I HOPE, YOU'LL, UNDER THE, FOR YOU, HERE TAKE, TO HIDDEN, FORGET YOUR, DETECTOR, THE BEACH, HOME, and HARRY.

"Again, it's just a bunch of random words," Marly said, studying the notebook.

"What if we swapped the pages?" Sai said. He carefully ripped out the pages of Marly's notebook and switched their order. Together, the papers read:

WELCOME TO	HOUSE
I HOPE	YOUR STAY
YOU'LL	BIKES
UNDER THE	THEY ARE
FOR YOU	WHILE YOU'RE
HERE TAKE	DOWN
TO HIDDEN	BEACH DON'T
FORGET YOUR	AND METAL
DETECTOR	GET TO
THE BEACH	YOURSELVES AT
HOME	SUMMERLING
HARRY	

"There's definitely another paper to find. And I bet it goes right in between these two papers," Isla said.

"Agreed," Marly said. "All that's missing between *Harry* and *Summerling* is a *P*."

"Well, let's see if we can find it," Sai said, hopping to his feet.

They searched drawers and cabinets all over the cabin. Upstairs and downstairs. They searched under furniture. Finally, Sai

lifted one of the bike helmets that hung on a
wall beside the front door. A paper with two
straight edges and two jagged edges fluttered
to the floor.

"Aha!" Sai said, picking it up. He turned it
over and revealed another message written
in dots. They raced back up the stairs and
gathered around the encyclopedia, which was
still open to the braille chart.

"First letter is an *S*," Sai said.

"Then a *U*," Isla said.

Now that they'd done this a couple of

times, Isla and Sai were faster at recognizing patterns. It didn't take nearly as long to decode this third paper: SUMMER, YOU ENJOY, FIND THREE, PORCH, TO USE, A RIDE, BAY, MAP SHOVEL, WHEN YOU, MAKE, and *P*.

When they put all three papers together in order, the jagged edges matched up perfectly. Marly wrote the full message, with proper punctuation, in their notebook while Isla read it out loud.

"'Welcome to Summer House. I hope you enjoy your stay. You'll find three bikes under the porch. They are for you to use while you're here. Take a ride down to Hidden Bay Beach. Don't forget your map, shovel, and metal detector. When

Welcome to Summer House. I hope you enjoy your stay. You'll find three bikes under the porch. They are for you to use while you're here. Take a ride down to Hidden Bay Beach. Don't forget your map, shovel, and metal detector. When you get to the beach, make yourselves at home.

Harry P. Summerling

you get to the beach, make yourselves at home. Harry P. Summerling.'"

Sai rubbed his hands together. "Guess we know what we have to do now: go to Hidden Bay Beach and dig for treasure!"

"Yeah, but where's Hidden Bay Beach?" Marly asked.

"Let's check the map," Isla said. "I think I left it in the ATV yesterday."

Marly closed the notebook and put it in her tote bag. Then they all trooped down the stairs and out the door.

Stella glanced up from her book as they raced past her on the porch. "Where are you three off to in such a hurry?" she asked.

"For now, we're just getting the map," Isla told Stella.

Sai hoisted himself through the window of the ATV's back seat. "Found it!" He waved it in the air and hopped back down to the ground.

Marly and Isla gathered around him. "There it is!" Marly pointed at Hidden Bay Beach on the map.

"There are supposed to be bikes under the porch," Sai said.

"Where?" Marly asked. The whole area under the front porch was blocked off with some sort of lattice fencing. Sai handed the map to Marly and she slipped it into her bag along with the notebook. Then they walked around behind the porch steps.

"There!" Isla said as a door came into view. She opened it and revealed a little storage space beneath the porch. There were several bikes tucked away under there, along with some old flowerpots, wire fencing, and gardening tools.

"A shovel," Sai said, grabbing it. "We need that, too. And your metal detector, Marly."

"That's in the cabin!" Marly said.

They wheeled the bikes out from under the

porch and then Marly ran inside to get her metal detector.

When she returned, Isla was asking Stella, "Is it okay if we ride these bikes to Hidden Bay Beach? That's what our puzzle says to do."

"Sure," Stella replied. "Maybe you want to make yourselves some sandwiches and have a picnic on the beach while you're there."

"That sounds nice," Marly said. "Assuming there actually *is* a beach there." They hadn't seen anything that Marly thought of as a "beach" since they'd arrived. The whole island seemed to be nothing but rocks and trees.

"I don't think it would be called Hidden Bay *Beach* if there wasn't a beach," Sai said.

"Well, let's find out!" Marly said.

Chapter 7

DIGGING FOR TREASURE

"See? Told you there'd be a beach," Sai said an hour later when they arrived at Hidden Bay Beach. He took off his helmet and hung it from his handlebars.

The tall evergreens had disappeared almost as soon as they took the turn toward Hidden Bay Beach. Now a wide, sandy beach scattered with large driftwood logs stretched before them. Marly grinned. This was what she'd expected Summer Island to be like.

She shaded her eye and gazed out at the

water. There was another, much smaller, island not too far from shore. It had a single tree on it.

"Look over there!" Sai pointed at a small driftwood structure near some tall grass down the beach.

"Oh wow," Marly said, taking a few steps toward it. "I wonder who built that."

"Mr. Summerling?" Sai suggested.

"You think?" Marly asked.

Sai shrugged. "Who else? Captain Joe said

there isn't anyone else on this island."

"We could eat our lunch in there and figure out what to do next," Isla said as she unfastened the picnic basket from her bike.

"We already know what to do next," Sai said. "Run the metal detector over the entire beach." He sighed. "It'll probably take us all afternoon to do that."

"At least we've *got* a metal detector," Marly said. "Imagine if we had to dig up this whole beach without one." They grabbed their things and trudged toward the driftwood structure. Sand quickly filled their shoes, but Marly didn't mind. The sun was bright. A warm breeze came in from the water. And the air smelled fresh and clean.

"This is so cool," Isla said, bending down to enter the structure. It was nice and shaded inside. All that was in there was a tree stump table and three tree stump stools.

"This reminds me of our tree house," Marly

said as she stowed her bag and metal detector in a corner.

"Me too!" Sai said. "Except the tree house has windows."

Marly kicked off her shoes, dumped out the sand, and tossed them over by her metal detector. Isla opened their picnic basket and passed around peanut butter and jelly sandwiches, chips, carrots, and apples.

"Have you ever noticed peanut butter and jelly sandwiches taste better outside?" Sai asked as they sat down to eat.

"Totally," Marly agreed.

Isla turned to Marly. "You brought our notebook, didn't you?"

"Of course," Marly said, her mouth full of peanut butter. She didn't go anywhere without their notebook. "It's in my bag. Why?"

"I want to see that three-part message again," Isla said.

Marly grabbed the notebook from her bag

and handed it to Isla. Isla immediately opened to the page she wanted and stared at it while she slowly chewed her apple.

Sai helped himself to a handful of chips. "What are you looking for?" he asked.

"This," Isla said finally. She set the notebook on the table and pointed at the line that read: MAKE YOURSELVES AT HOME. "What is this?" She gestured all around them. "Where are we?"

"In a house?" Sai's voice rose like he was asking a question.

"A home," Isla corrected.

"Oh," Marly said, curling her toes in the sand. "We don't need to walk the metal detector across the whole beach. What we're looking for is probably somewhere in here. Buried in the sand." That wasn't such a large area to search.

Sai kicked over his stool in his rush to get to the metal detector. "How do you turn this thing on again?"

Marly showed him where the On/Off switch was, and the machine let out a low hum as soon as he turned it on. He swept it back and forth in wide arcs across the sand.

"Go slower," Marly suggested.

Sai slowed down. He crept across the sand, holding the metal detector like it was a dog on a leash in front of him. All of a sudden, the noise from the machine grew louder and more high-pitched. Then, just as quickly, it returned to a low hum.

"Go back!" Isla waved him backward. "I think there was something there."

Sai took two steps backward and the high-pitched noise returned. He turned off the metal detector and leaned it against the wall. "We need to dig right here," he said, stomping on the sand.

Marly grabbed the shovel and started digging. Isla and Sai helped with their hands. Their hole was about a foot deep when Marly felt her shovel strike metal. She dug some more and uncovered a familiar-looking blue metal box.

"That must be the treasure!" Sai helped Marly pull it from the sand. "I can't believe we found it already."

"Don't be too sure about that," Isla said, sitting back on her heels. "It could just be another puzzle."

Marly unclipped the box and lifted the lid. Inside was a single sheet of paper. She found it odd that, like the clues they'd found in the cabin, it didn't have the *From the Desk of Harry P. Summerling* header. But no doubt about it. This was another puzzle.

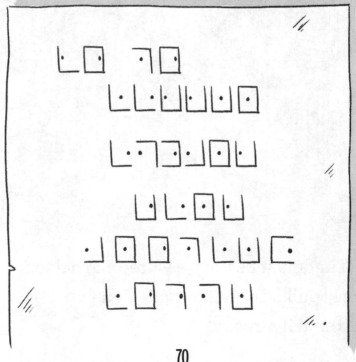

"Yay! We know how to solve that one," Sai said, rubbing his hands together.

"We do?" Isla twisted her hair.

"Yes! Don't you recognize it?" Sai tilted his head in surprise. "It's that tic-tac-toe code that we found in the phone booth outside my parents' store." That was way back when they were searching for the first treasure.

"No, that was pigpen." Isla shook her head. "This doesn't look like pigpen to me. There are no X's in it."

"What do you mean, 'no X's'?" Sai asked.

Marly knew what Isla meant. She grabbed the notebook and flipped pages until she found the one where they'd worked out the pigpen code. "Remember? We wrote all the letters of the alphabet inside tic-tac-toe boards *and* X's. Isla's right. This isn't the same code. Unless there are no *S, T, U, V, W, X, Y,* or *Z*s in the whole message."

Sai shrugged. "Maybe there aren't."

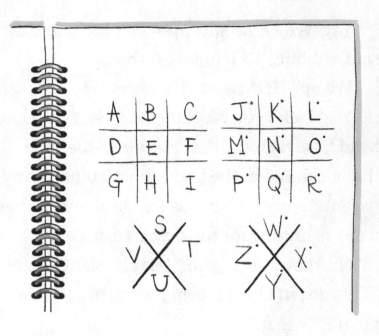

"Easy enough to find out," Isla said. "The first letter matches the upper right corner of a tic-tic-toe board. The one with the dot in it." She held the new code next to the pigpen key in their notebook.

"That's *L*," Marly said. She marked the pigpen code page with one hand while turning to a blank page with the other hand. She put an *L* on the blank page.

"Next one is a square with a dot," Sai said.

Marly checked the pigpen page. "That would be an *N*," she said. "So, *L-N*?" She scratched her forehead. "That's not a word."

"Wait a minute," Sai took a closer look at the new puzzle. "*All* of these symbols have dots in them. Do you see that?"

"Yeah. I think Isla's right. This isn't pigpen," Marly said. She crossed out the *L* and the *N* and set her pencil down.

Isla twisted her allergy bracelet. "It could be something similar, though," she said.

Sai's foot twitched. "Sometimes the dot is way on the left, sometimes it's in the middle, and sometimes it's way on the right," he said.

"So?" Marly said.

"So, maybe it still has something to do with tic-tac-toe," Sai said. He took the notebook from Marly. "What if we draw it like this?" He drew a tic-tac-toe board that took up the whole page, then put an *A*, *B*, and *C* in the top left square, a *D*, *E*, and *F* in the top

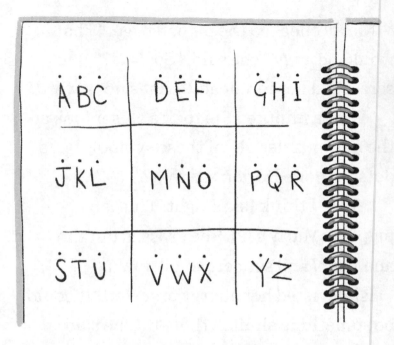

middle square, and a *G*, *H*, and *I* in the top right square. He kept going until he ran out of letters in the bottom right square. "Okay, maybe not," he said with disappointment. "There's only two letters left for the last square."

"It's still worth checking out," Marly said, glancing back and forth between the puzzle and Sai's tic-tac-toe board.

"Agreed," Isla said. "That first symbol looks

like the top right box and the dot is way over to the left, which would make this first letter a *G*."

Marly wrote a *G* below the first character of the code.

"Next one is an *O*," Sai said.

Marly put an *O* below the second character. *This is already looking better*, she thought.

"Then *T*," Isla said.

"Another *O*," Sai said.

"I think this is right," Isla said.

Marly nodded.

They continued letter by letter. When they finished, the message read: GO TO HIDDEN ISLAND FIND ANOTHER HOUSE.

Chapter 8

THE TURNING TIDE

S ai left the driftwood house and tromped through the loose sand. "I bet that's the hidden island right over there." He stood at the edge of the water and pointed at the small island with the tree.

Isla and Marly hurried over to him. "You think so?" Isla said, shading her eyes.

"It's not exactly hidden," Marly pointed out.

"Well, it's right by Hidden Bay Beach," Sai said. "And if you're out on the ocean on the other side of this island, you wouldn't be able

to see it. So *then* it would be hidden, right?"

Marly thought that was a bit of a stretch, but they also didn't have any other leads. "How do we get there? It's too far to swim."

Just then, a freezing-cold wave washed over their feet.

"Ahh!" They all screamed and leaped back out of the water.

"It's also too *cold* to swim!" Isla said.

"We need a boat," Sai said.

"I don't know," Marly said. She didn't like the idea of the three of them paddling a boat by themselves. Weren't there currents in the ocean?

Isla didn't like that idea any better than Marly did. "That seems dangerous," she said. "Remember what happened to Mr. Summerling?"

"Yeah. He got caught in a storm," Sai said. "But it's not going to storm now." He tipped his head back and let the sun warm his face. "There isn't a cloud in the sky."

"Maybe not," Marly said. "But we still could end up way out in the ocean."

"We could," Isla agreed.

Sai wrinkled his nose. "Well, we don't have a boat anyway," he grumbled.

They gazed at the water and the island, each lost in their own thoughts. There had to be a way to get over to that island. A safe way.

Marly watched the waves come in and go out. Which gave her an idea! "Hey, this is the ocean, so there are tides, right?" she said. "Maybe we have to wait for the tide to go out, and then we'll be able to walk there."

"Oh, I saw that in a movie once," Sai said.

Isla crossed her arms. "I don't think the tide is going to go out that far," she said. "If it does, it'll take hours."

"Or you know what else could happen?" Sai's eyes gleamed with excitement. "Maybe there's an island we can't see right now because it's under water, but when the tide goes out, it'll show up?"

"That would be pretty cool," Marly said.

"Now *that* would be a 'hidden' island," Isla said.

"Why don't we hang around for a while and see if anything changes with the tide," Marly suggested.

"Ack!" Sai shrieked as he darted to the side, practically knocking Isla over.

"What?" she asked, rubbing her elbow.

"B-bee!" Sai pointed and Isla slowly backed away.

Marly squinted. "Where?"

"Uh . . . ," Sai said, looking around. "I don't see it anymore."

"Neither do I," Marly said.

"Hey, I'm the one who's allergic to bee stings, remember?" Isla raised her arm so Sai could see her allergy bracelet. "But you're the one screaming and running into people?"

"I may not be allergic, but I still don't want to get stung," Sai said.

"No one does," Marly said. But if there were any bees hanging around, neither she nor Isla ever saw them.

For the next few hours, the three of them ran up and down the beach, built a sandcastle, and when they got tired from the sun, they went back inside the little driftwood house.

"Is it my imagination or is the water getting higher rather than lower?" Sai asked.

"It's definitely getting higher," Marly said. "Look at our sandcastle." The water lapped closer and closer to it.

"This is fun, but I don't think we're ever going to be able to walk to that island," Isla said with disappointment.

"And I don't see any new islands appearing in the water," Marly said. "Maybe we should go back to the cabin and make a new plan."

"Fine," Sai said. "I'm getting hungry again anyway." But Marly could tell he hadn't fully given up on that island.

Back at the cabin, Marly, Isla, and Sai helped Stella make tacos, chips, and guacamole for dinner. While they were cooking, the kids told Stella all about the driftwood house they'd discovered at Hidden Bay Beach, the metal box that was buried in the sand, and the puzzle they'd found inside.

"Maybe it's just me, but figuring out how to solve the puzzles seems easier this time around," Sai said as he mashed an avocado with the back of a fork. "It's the next part that's hard."

Marly glanced up from the cheese she was grating. "That's true," she said.

"What do you mean by 'the next part'?" Stella put the taco shells in the oven and set the timer.

Isla went to get their notebook. "Here's our latest puzzle," she said. She pulled out the paper with the solved code and showed it to Stella.

"'Go to hidden island, find another house,'" Stella read.

"We solved the puzzle pretty easily, but we have no idea where the hidden island is," Marly said.

"There's a little island not far from shore on Hidden Bay Beach," Sai explained. "I still think that's it, but we can't get to it. Unless you know where there's a boat we could take."

Stella shook her head. "I don't think Harry would want you all in a small boat out on the ocean," she said.

"That's what we said," Marly chimed in.

Sai groaned.

"Cheer up, Sai," Isla said. "I really don't think that's the hidden island."

"Then where is it?" Sai threw his hands in the air.

"I don't know," Isla said.

"You'll find it," Stella said with confidence. "I know you will."

Marly hoped Stella was right. They only had two more full days on Summer Island. And no idea how many more puzzles there were to solve.

Chapter 9

A NEW IDEA

"What should we do today?" Isla asked as they cleared their breakfast dishes the next morning.

"Find the hidden island," Sai said.

"Duh," Marly said. "How are we going to do that?" She set her dishes in the sink, then went to get their map of the island. She spread it out on the counter, and Isla and Sai peered over her shoulder.

"We could start by following Main Path," Isla said. "We haven't been to this part of the island at all." She waved her hand over the whole northeast part of the map.

"While we're over that way, we should also check out this lake." Sai slapped it on the map. "And look! There's an island smack dab in the middle of it."

"It's not exactly hidden if it's on the map," Marly pointed out.

"It's still worth checking out," Isla said.

"Sounds like you know what you're doing today," Stella said. "I think I'll be spending another morning on the porch. I'm really starting to get into this 'vacation' thing."

The kids helped Stella with the dishes, then headed outside. It was another crisp morning. Isla tucked a small bag into her bike basket.

"Do we need the metal detector?" Marly asked.

"We've still got our shovel from yesterday," Sai said, pointing to his bike basket.

"If we need the metal detector, we can

come back and get it," Isla said. "For now, let's just explore."

They got on their bikes and started pedaling. When they got to Main Path, they turned right, and kept going past the turn-off to Hidden Bay Beach. They'd never been this far on Main Path, but once again, all they saw were trees, trees, and more trees. Finally, they came to a sign that said Lake. An arrow pointed the way.

"Should we turn?" Isla asked over her shoulder.

"Do it!" Sai said, zooming ahead of her.

This trail was muddier than Main Path, and Marly needed to watch where she was going so she didn't get stuck or wipe out.

About a quarter of a mile down the trail, they arrived at a lake that was so still, it looked like glass. And there, in the middle of the lake, was an island covered in trees.

"What do you think?" Sai asked, leaning on his handlebars. "Could that be the hidden island?"

"It's kind of hidden," Isla said. "This whole lake is surrounded by trees."

"Same problem as before. How do we get there?" Marly asked.

There was a dock ahead. A green-and-blue flag rose from a pole at the end of it. But there was no boat in sight.

"I wonder how cold *that* water is," Sai said

as they got off their bikes. "Maybe we could swim over."

"I don't know," Marly said nervously.

"We don't know what's in that lake or how deep it is," Isla said.

"Fine," Sai said, letting out a big breath. "Let's at least go out onto the dock and get a closer look." He raced ahead of the girls, right through a patch of tall grass and daisies.

Marly and Isla both sighed at the same

time, then followed Sai. Marly had to admit that his excitement was contagious.

But when they got close to the water, Isla suddenly stopped. Something off to the right had caught her attention. "What is that?" she asked.

Marly turned. "What is what?" She squinted. "Oh, that box or whatever on that post? I'll go see." She jogged across the sand.

Sai wasn't paying any attention to Marly. He stood at the end of the dock, peering at the island. But Isla watched Marly intently.

"It's a telephone!" Marly yelled to the others.

"Really?" That got Sai's attention. "Out here?" He clomped down the dock, and he and Isla ran toward Marly.

"Maybe we're supposed to call someone for a ride to the island?" Isla suggested.

"Who?" Sai asked.

Marly picked up the receiver and put it to her ear. "No dial tone," she said, hanging up. "So calling someone is out."

Then she noticed
something else. Behind
Isla and Sai. Past the
dock. She squinted.

"What is *that*?" she asked, staring at a tree
that was bent over the water. Was there some
sort of picture carved into that tree?

The three friends ran over. "It's a carving of
a bear," Isla said, shading her eyes.

Marly stopped beside the patch of daisies.
"It reminds me of the bears outside the
library at home," she said. The Sandford
Public Library had carved statues of Mama
Bear and Little Bear outside. In fact, Marly,
Isla, and Sai had solved one of their earliest
puzzles there.

"Wait a minute," Sai said, turning around
in a circle. "Bear. Telephone. Daisies. Where
have we seen these things before?"

"In the tree house *and* in the tower room

at Mr. Summerling's house," Marly said. "But we're missing a globe." The other two times they'd come upon pictures of a bear, a telephone, daisies, and a globe, they had needed to "make a T." They'd imagined lines running between the four objects, and right where those lines crossed, they'd discovered something hidden below. Both times.

"Maybe there's a globe on that flag?" Isla said. "There's no wind so I can't tell what's on it." The flag hung limply against the pole.

Sai climbed back up onto the dock and ran all the way to the end. He stood on his tiptoes and stretched his arm as high as he could, but he wasn't tall enough to reach the flag. He tried jumping, but still couldn't reach it.

"Let's assume it's a globe," Marly said. She found the spot where imaginary lines between the bear, telephone, daisies, and the flag at the end of the dock came together on the sand. "We should dig here!"

"I'll go get the shovel," Sai said, barreling back down the dock.

Isla dropped to her knees beside Marly and they started digging with their hands. Sai returned with the shovel. He crowded in between them and made their hole deeper and deeper. It wasn't long before they heard the familiar clang of metal hitting metal. And a few minutes later, they pulled out another metal box.

They opened it up and found a paper inside. It read:

Blf droo urmw z ylzg zg Nroovi Ozmwrmt

Chapter 10

ILSA'S IN TROUBLE

"Great. Another code," Sai said in a tired voice.

"Don't worry. We've still got plenty of time to finish this treasure hunt," Marly said.

"I'm not worried," Sai said. "I—"

"Ouch!" Isla yelped and slapped at her arm. Her eyes grew large. "Oh no. No, no, no . . ." The color drained from her face.

94

"What?" Marly turned to Isla.

"I-I—" Isla dropped onto the sand. Her eyes were red and watery. Her face and neck were swelling like a balloon.

Marly gaped. "Did you just get stung by a bee?"

"I-I—" Isla nodded.

Sai's mouth fell open. "B-but you're allergic to bees," he said.

Isla couldn't talk. She was struggling to breathe.

Sai grabbed Marly's arm. "What do we do? What do we do?"

Marly's heart felt like it might explode from her chest. She didn't know what to do!

"Go get Stella," she said finally.

Sai bolted for his bike.

Marly couldn't tear her eyes away from the angry red splotch on Isla's forearm. It was growing larger by the second. *Stay calm!* she told herself. But that was easier said than done.

Isla clung to Marly's arm. Tears ran down her swollen face. "Ep-ep-ep," she gasped.

"EpiPen?" Marly guessed. "You need your EpiPen?"

Isla nodded.

"Where is it?" Marly asked, looking around. Obviously, it wasn't here in the sand. Had she even brought it?

Isla raised a shaky hand, but Marly didn't understand what she was trying to do.

"I DON'T KNOW WHERE IT IS!" Marly cried. Tears of frustration filled her eyes. Then she realized Isla was trying to show her.

"On your bike?" Marly asked.

Isla nodded. A horrible rasping, wheezing sound came from her mouth.

Marly ran to the bikes. There was a bag in the front basket on Isla's bike. Marly grabbed it and hurried back to her friend. "Is it in here?" She didn't wait for an answer. She dumped the whole bag out onto the sand.

Isla grabbed one of the green tubes and shoved it at Marly's chest.

Marly shrank back. "You want *me* to do it?"

Isla nodded desperately.

"I don't know what to do with an EpiPen!" *Where are Sai and Stella?*

Isla pounded the tube against her thigh, then pushed it at Marly again, her eyes wild with fear.

Tears poured down Marly's cheeks. She didn't have a choice. She had to do this. She knew what could happen to Isla if she didn't.

She took the EpiPen. *Thank goodness, there are directions right on it!* She moved her eye patch so she could read the directions clearly. There were only three steps.

I can do this, Marly told herself. She flipped open the green cap and slid the device out. Then she popped the blue cap. The only thing left to do was inject it. She put one hand on Isla's thigh, took a deep breath, and jabbed the orange end of the tube into Isla's leg. There was a short click. Marly held it there for three seconds like the directions said, then pulled it out.

Her heart raced. She met Isla's eyes. Was that it? Was that all she had to do?

Marly turned the tube around in her hand. She didn't see any needle. Was it inside the orange thing? There was still liquid rolling around in there. *Uh-oh.* Maybe she hadn't done it right.

"Do we need to do it again?" she asked.

Isla shook her head and started rubbing the spot on her leg where Marly had injected the medicine.

"Does it hurt?" Marly asked.

"Yeah," Isla said.

Stupid question, Marly thought. Of course, it hurt to get a needle shoved into your thigh.

Marly was still worried about that liquid inside the tube. "Um," she said. "We didn't get all the liquid out. Are you sure we don't have to do it again?"

Isla was still breathing really hard. "I-it . . . doesn't all . . . come . . . out," she said.

"Oh. Okay." So Marly *had* done it right. That was a relief.

"Maybe you shouldn't talk," she said, patting Isla's non-stung arm. "Just rest. Sai went to get Stella."

"Good." Isla nodded. Her eyelids looked heavy.

She's not going to pass out or anything, is she? Marly wondered. "Are you feeling better?" she asked, forgetting she'd just told Isla not to talk. But it seemed like the swelling on her face and throat was going down.

"Yeah," Isla said.

A few minutes later, Marly heard a vehicle. Then Stella's voice: "Marly? Isla?"

Finally! Marly thought. "We're over here," she called as Stella and Sai flew toward them.

Isla tried to sit up. "I-I'm okay," she told Stella. "Marly . . . used my . . . EpiPen."

Stella crouched down beside Isla. "If Marly had to use your EpiPen on you, you most certainly are *not* okay," she said. "And without cell phone service, I'm not sure what to do." She said the last part under her breath, almost like she was talking to herself.

"I'm feeling better," Isla said.

"How many times have you been stung by a bee?" Sai asked.

"Three," Isla replied.

"What do you do when that happens?" Stella asked.

"I . . . don't really remember . . . the first time . . . ," Isla panted. "Last time my mom gave me my EpiPen . . . then called 9-1-1 . . . and we went to the hospital . . ."

Stella's eyebrows knit together with concern.

"B-b-but I didn't have to stay at the hospital," Isla went on. "They didn't have to give me any more medicine . . . I really am feeling better now." She managed a small smile. "I'm just . . . tired."

"Well," Stella said finally, "let's get you back to the cabin and we can figure out what to do from there." She put her hands under Isla's body, but Isla wiggled away.

"I can walk," she said. "I just . . . have to go slow."

Marly and Stella helped Isla to her feet and walked her slowly over to the ATV. After getting her settled in the back seat, Marly said, "What about the bikes?" Sai had ridden his back to the cabin, but the other two were still here. And they were too big and awkward to put in the back of the ATV.

"You and I can ride them back," Sai said, elbowing Marly.

Stella nodded. "Yes, why don't you do that," she said. "We'll see you back at the cabin."

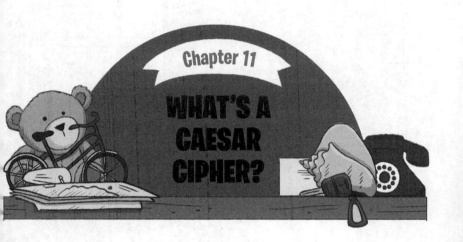

Chapter 11

WHAT'S A CAESAR CIPHER?

Isla yawned and stretched on the sofa.

"She's awake," Sai announced as Isla's eyes fluttered open.

Stella set her book on the table and Marly scooted forward on her chair. "How are you feeling?" Marly asked.

Isla seemed a little stunned by all the attention. "Fine. Just tired. I was tired after the last time I got stung, too. What time is it?" The swelling in her face and neck was completely gone and her face was a normal color.

"Almost five o'clock," Sai said.

"I slept all day?" Isla said with dismay.

"It's okay," Marly said, patting her leg.

"You needed the sleep," Stella said.

"But the treasure hunt." Isla's bottom lip quivered. "We wasted the whole day. Unless you two solved the new puzzle. Did you?" She looked up hopefully at Marly and Sai.

"Of course not," Marly said.

"We waited for you," Sai added.

Isla tossed her blanket aside. "Then, let's get to work." She started to sit up.

"Hold on there," Stella said. "Your health is far more important than any treasure hunt. Your parents are going to have my head on a silver platter when they hear about this." She tried to guide Isla back down on the sofa, but Isla refused to lie down.

She grabbed her cat ears and plopped them on her head. "I'm okay. Really!" she insisted. "I had my medicine. I had a nap. My arm doesn't really even hurt anymore." She slapped her arm lightly to prove her point.

Stella looked doubtful.

"We read about bee sting allergies in the encyclopedia," Sai said. "Marly saved your life!"

"Thanks, Marly," Isla said.

Marly blushed. "I'm glad you're feeling better," she said.

"Can we please, please, please work on the puzzle?" Isla begged Stella. "I promise I'm well enough to do that, and it'll take my mind off the bee sting."

"We only have one more day here," Sai pointed out.

Marly could tell how badly Isla wanted to work on the puzzle. And she seemed better. "We won't let her work too hard," Marly told Stella.

Stella pressed her lips together. "You can work on the puzzle as long as Isla doesn't leave the sofa," she said finally. "And while you're doing that, I'll go see what there is for dinner."

Sai sat down beside Isla. "I bet we're close to the end of this treasure hunt," he said.

"Really?" Marly said. "What makes you say that?"

"We had to make a T! That always comes at the end," Sai said, confidently.

"Hmm," Marly said. Sai was right. Drawing imaginary lines between globes and bears and daisies and telephones was always the last thing they did. "But we've still got at least one more puzzle to solve."

"Maybe the treasure hunt ends on the island in the middle of the lake, and the puzzle tells us how to get there," Isla suggested.

"I bet that's it," Sai said.

"Where's the puzzle?" Isla looked around.

Marly went to get her notebook where she'd stuffed the clue, and brought it back to the sofa. Then they all huddled close together, studying the new paper.

Blf droo urmw z ylzg zg Nroovi Ozmwrmt

"Is it a Caesar cipher?" Isla asked.

"What's that? Have we had that one before?" Sai asked.

"It's where you shift the position of each letter in the alphabet," Isla explained. "It's easier to show you than tell you."

She took the notebook from Marly, opened

to a clean page, and wrote out the alphabet. Then she wrote it again right below the first alphabet, but this time she started with *B*. She put the *B* below the *A*, a *C* below the *B*, a *D* below the *C* . . . and when she got to *Z*, she put an *A* below it.

A B C D E F G H I
B C D E F G H I J

J K L M N O P
K L M N O P Q

Q R S T U V W
R S T U V W X

X Y Z
Y Z A

"This is our key," Isla said. "If we go back to the puzzle, *B-L-F* becomes *C* . . . *M* . . . *G* . . . which is not a word."

"No, it's not," Marly said, holding her chin in her hands.

"It's fine," Isla said. "We might have to shift it more than one space. So instead of *A* equals *B*, maybe *A* equals *C*." She turned to the next page and wrote out a whole new key, starting with *C* this time, and ending with an *A* below the *Y* and a *B* below the *Z*. Then she tried to decode the first word of the puzzle again. "D ... N ... H?" she said.

"Still not a word," Marly said.

"Okay. We'll shift it again," Isla said.

"Are we going to do this twenty-six times?" Sai slumped back against the sofa.

"No," Marly said. "We don't have to do it twenty-six times. Look at the *Z*. How many one-letter words are there in the English language?"

"Two," Isla said with a slow smile. "*A* and *I*."

"So ... we only need to do this two more times," Sai said, catching on. "Once where *Z* is an *A* and once where *Z* is an *I*."

"Actually, we only need to do it *one* more

time," Isla said. "We already did *Z* equals *A*. See?" She turned back to their first key to show Sai.

"*Ohhh,*" Sai said, sitting back up again.

Isla wrote out one more alphabet. She put an *I* below the *Z*, a *J* below the *A*, and so on until she got all the way up to *Y*.

Marly felt excitement swelling within her as she watched Isla write *K . . . U . . . O . . .*

Isla groaned. "Still not right."

"Aww," Marly said. "I was sure that was it."

Sai closed his eyes and started mouthing something while he counted on his fingers.

"What are you doing, Sai?" Isla asked.

"Shh!" Sai held up a finger.

Marly and Isla shrugged at each other.

All of a sudden, Sai leaped to his feet. "That's it! It's a backward alphabet! The first word is 'you'!"

Marly nudged Isla. "Try it," she said.

Isla wrote out the alphabet again. Then she

wrote it again, backward, right below the first
alphabet.

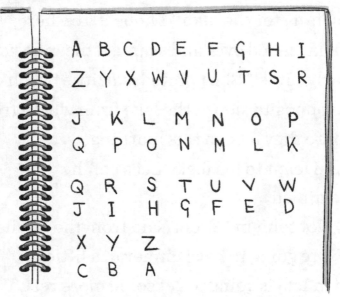

Letter by letter, they decoded the whole
puzzle. When they finished, it read:

YOU WILL FIND A BOAT AT MILLER LANDING

"I knew it!" Sai pumped his fist in the air.
"That island in the middle of the lake *is* our
hidden island. Now all we have to do is find
the boat so we can go there, find the house,

and hopefully find our treasure!"

"Where's Miller Landing?" Marly asked, reaching for the map. "I hope it's on here."

Isla leaned over and scanned the map with Marly. "It is!" She pointed at a little beach on the opposite side of the lake from where from where they'd been this morning.

Sai leapt to his feet. "Let's go!" he exclaimed.

"Not tonight," Stella said from the kitchen. "We're going to have dinner in a little bit. Then Isla is going to get some more rest. We'll see it tomorrow."

Marly sighed, but she knew there'd be no changing Stella's mind. Not while Isla was still recovering. She hoped Sai was right and the treasure hunt was almost over. Otherwise, they may not be able to finish before Captain Joe came back for them. *Not finishing is not an option*, she said to herself.

Chapter 12

SURPRISE

In the morning, Marly, Isla, and Sai mapped out a route to Miller Landing.

Stella held up the ATV key. "The only way I'm going to let you three continue this treasure hunt is if I come along," she said firmly.

Marly, Isla, and Sai exchanged surprised looks.

"But you're not supposed to help us," Sai said. "That's what you said when we first got here."

"I'm not going to help you with the puzzles. I'm just going to drive you where you need to go. That way I can make sure everyone is safe," Stella said with a pointed look at Isla. "Vacation is officially over."

"We'll get there faster in an ATV than on bikes," Marly pointed out.

"Let's go!" Isla grabbed the map and headed for the door.

While Stella drove, Marly and Isla followed along on the map and told her where to turn.

"What is Miller Landing, anyway?" Sai asked.

"We're about to find out," Isla said as they approached a wooden sign that pointed the way to Miller Landing.

Stella turned and followed the narrow trail through the trees. It came to a dead end at a small clearing on the lake. There were no buildings and no dock. But lying upside down on the sand was a small rowboat.

Everyone got out of the ATV and ran toward the boat.

Marly shaded her eye. "I hope there are oars," she said. They all got on one side of the boat to flip it over.

"Yay, oars!" Isla said as the boat plopped down right side up on the sand. There were two oars clipped to the inside of the boat, and four life jackets tucked beneath the seats.

"Hey, the place where Isla got stung is right over there." Sai pointed across the lake.

Marly squinted. She could barely make out a dock with a flag.

Isla winced. "How about we call it 'the place where we made the T' instead?"

"Okay," Sai agreed. They bumped fists.

"Let's get this boat in the lake," Marly said. She couldn't wait to see what was on that island.

"First the life jackets," Stella said sternly. After yesterday, she clearly wasn't taking any chances.

They each grabbed a life jacket and put

it on. Then they slipped off their shoes and tossed them into the boat.

Marly helped Stella drag the front end of the boat into the water, and Isla and Sai pushed from behind.

"Ah!" Marly shrieked as her foot came down in the cold water.

"I don't think it's as cold as the other beach," Sai said.

"Cold is cold," Isla said. Then they all climbed into the boat.

Sai claimed one of the oars, Marly grabbed the other, and they started paddling. The water was calm, but Marly and Sai had a hard time getting the boat to go where they wanted it to go.

"You two need to work together," Stella told them.

Marly and Sai watched each other and tried to paddle together. Eventually, they found a rhythm. As they drew closer to the island, they saw a sign planted in the sand. It read Hidden Island.

"Look!" Isla said with excitement.

Marly and Sai turned their heads.

"Aha!" Sai cried, rocking the boat. "We were never looking for *a* hidden island. We were looking for an island *called* Hidden Island."

"And look! There's a house." Marly pointed. "I bet our next clue is in there."

"Hopefully it's our *last* clue," Sai said.

"I wonder what the treasure is this time," Isla said.

Knowing that Mr. Summerling always had an extra surprise up his sleeve, Marly couldn't even begin to guess.

As soon as Sai's oar touched sand, he scrambled out of the boat. It lurched from side to side.

"Wait, Sai," Marly said as he stomped and splashed through the water.

"Yes, hold on, Sai," Stella said. "We need to pull the boat far enough onto the sand so that it can't float away. We don't want to be stranded here."

Marly, Isla, and Stella got out of the boat. But Sai kept right on going.

"Hey!" Marly yelled with her hands on her hips. "It's not fair for you to see what's on this island before the rest of us do."

"Sorry, sorry," he said, turning back. "I'm just excited."

Together, they dragged the boat across the sand and up onto the grass. Then they all put on their shoes and marched up to the cabin. It was nothing like the cabin where they were staying. This one was much smaller. The porch sagged and some of the wood was rotting.

"It's like a pioneer cabin," Isla said.

"I wonder if anyone ever lived here," Marly said.

"Be careful," Stella said when Sai tried the door. Surprisingly enough, it creaked open! They all stepped inside.

"It really is a pioneer cabin," Isla said, looking around in wonder. It was a one-room cabin. The only light inside was the natural light that came in through the two windows. There was a single unmade bed that maybe doubled as a sofa, a small cook stove, and

a table with two chairs. On the table was
another blue metal box just waiting for them.

"Treasure!" Sai cried. They all rushed over
and Marly lifted the lid.

Ilsa gasped.

Inside the box was an old spyglass and a
book on the history of secret codes.

"Cool!" Sai said, reaching for the spyglass.
He put it to his eye, then frowned. "I can't see
anything."

"You have to focus it," Stella said.

While Sai, Isla, and Stella tried to figure out

how to work the spyglass, Marly picked up the book and riffled through it. "This would've been helpful when we were trying to figure out what some of those codes were," she said.

Then she noticed the folded sheet of paper at the bottom of the box. "There's another letter," she said as she opened it up. "And this one's 'From the Desk of Harry P. Summerling'!"

But everyone else seemed more interested in the spyglass than the letter.

"Fine, I'll just read it myself," Marly muttered. The type was too small to read in the dim light, so she took it over to the window. She skimmed the page, and her breath caught in her throat.

"What?" Isla's head popped up. "What does it say?"

Marly's hesitation caused Sai and Stella to take notice, too.

"Marly?" Stella peered at her with concern.

"Uh . . ." Marly's hands began to shake. "It

says, 'Guess what, Treasure Troop. I'm alive!'"

"It says *what*?" Stella's eyes were wide with shock.

"He's alive?" Sai gaped. "For real?"

Marly remembered when Sai had brought up the possibility that Mr. Summerling could still be alive a couple weeks ago. None of them had really believed it.

"Is there more?" Stella asked intently.

Isla walked over and took Marly's hand.

"Yes, sorry," Marly said. She kept reading. "'Give the spyglass to Captain Joe when he returns for you—'"

"Aww!" Sai groaned.

"'He'll give you something in return. The book is yours to keep. I hope you've enjoyed your visit to Summer Island.'" Marly turned the paper over to see if there was anything else. "And that seems to be it."

"Did you know Mr. Summerling was alive?" Isla asked Stella.

"No," Stella breathed, still looking dazed. "I had no idea."

"Now what?" Sai said, setting the spyglass down. "Do we get to see him? Is he going to tell us why he let everyone think he was dead? And why do we have to give the spyglass to Captain Joe? We found it!"

"The letter says he'll give us something in return," Marly said. "I wonder what it is."

"Guess we'll find out tomorrow," Isla said.

Marly wasn't sure she could wait that long, but what choice did they have? "Hey, at least we finished the treasure hunt," she said. *And Mr. Summerling is alive!*

"Of course we finished the treasure hunt," Sai said. "The Treasure Troop rocks!"

Marly couldn't disagree with that.

The next morning, they packed their things,

closed up the cabin, and Stella drove the ATV back to the garage where they'd found it. Then they headed back down to the dock to wait for Captain Joe.

Marly squinted at the water, then gasped. "Was that—did you see that?" She wasn't positive, but she thought she saw a splash of water shoot up into the air like a fountain.

A few minutes later, she knew for sure. It was a whale! It leaped out of the water, then splashed back down headfirst.

"Oh wow!" Isla stared wide-eyed.

"So cool!" Sai said.

"Here comes Captain Joe," Stella said as a large boat motored toward them.

Would Captain Joe tell them where Mr. Summerling was? Would he take them to him? Marly couldn't wait to find out.

THE END